YETI AND THE BIRD

Nadia Shireen

JONATHAN CAPE • LONDON

YETI AND THE BIRD
A JONATHAN CAPE BOOK
978 1 780 08014 7

Published in Great Britain
by Jonathan Cape, an imprint
of Random House Children's Publishers
A Random House Group Company

This edition published 2013

10 9 8 7 6 5 4 3

RANDOM HOUSE CHILDREN'S PUBLISHERS UK
61–63 Uxbridge Road, London W5 5SA

www.**randomhousechildrens**.co.uk
www.**randomhouse**.co.uk

Addresses for companies within
The Random House Group Limited can be found at:
www.randomhouse.co.uk/offices.htm

THE RANDOM HOUSE GROUP
Limited Reg. No. 954009

A CIP catalogue record for this book is available
from the British Library.

Printed in China

For Najma Aunty and Rashid Uncle –
Mum and Khaloo Jaan.

Deep in the forest
there lived a yeti.

He was the

BIGGEST,
hairiest,
SCARIEST

beast anyone
had ever seen.

So everyone
left him alone.

But Yeti was lonely.

Then one day...

THUNK!

something

landed

on his head.

It was a bird.

And this little bird
didn't seem scared
of Yeti at all.

Sqwalka-
Sqwalka-
Sqwalka!

Not one BIT.

Instead,
the bird told
Yeti all about
her journey.

She seemed to think
she had landed on a
hot, tropical island
for the winter.

"Grooo?" said Yeti.

And sure enough, when the bird looked for sunshine and palm trees, there weren't any . . . She was lost.

The bird stopped
bouncing and chirping.

PAT PAT PAT

Yeti wasn't sure what to do
with the sad little thing.

After a while, he
decided to pick up
the bird and take
her home.

The next day, the forest
woke to a peculiar sight.

Yeti and the bird were playing!

And Yeti was laughing with a hearty roar nobody had heard before.

Every evening, the friends
sang sweet, sad songs together,
which soothed the forest to sleep.

Yeti wished the bird
could stay for ever.

But it was getting colder,
and he knew that soon
his small friend would
need to fly away.

So Yeti carefully examined
the bird's map, and found out
where she needed to go.

Then he made sure she was packed and ready for the long journey ahead.

Yeti sighed. Without the bird,
he was even lonelier than before.

Until . . .

. . . some new friends
came out to play.

THUD!

Deep in the forest
there lives a yeti,
with all his friends.

And every now and then,
the bird pops by to say hello.